C000002372

The Bird
of the Golden Land

by

ROBERT NYE

Illustrated by

KRYSTYNA TURSKA

HAMISH HAMILTON · London

To John Horder

First published in Great Britain 1980 by
Hamish Hamilton Childrens Books
Garden House, 57/59 Long Acre, London WC2E 9JZ

Text copyright © 1980 by Robert Nye
Illustrations copyright © 1980 by Krystyna Turska

Nye, Robert
    The bird of the golden land.
    I. Title
    823'.9'1J   PZ7.N99
    ISBN 0–241–10315–0

Printed in Great Britain

ONCE UPON A TIME, and a long time ago it was too, there used to be a hole in the middle of Ireland. At the bottom of this hole was a place called the Golden Land. One day a bird from the Golden Land came up this hole and started flying about in the world. The eyes of the bird were green and her feathers were gold. The bird sang as she flew. She flew high and she flew low. When she flew high she sang high and when she flew low she sang low. No one in the world had ever heard anything like it, the song was so sweet.

The bird of the Golden Land flew over thicket and thorn until she came to the castle of the King of Ireland. It was a castle full of cobwebs but it had nice window-sills. The bird of the Golden Land stood on the window-sill of the King's bedroom and fluffed up her gold feathers and started to sing. Her standing still song was even sweeter than her flying about song, because when she was standing still she sang both high and low in the same breath. The song of the bird of the Golden Land made the King of Ireland dream that he was very happy.

3

However, when the King of Ireland woke up and put on his crown he remembered that he had no reason to be happy at all. The King of Ireland had problems. The chief of his problems was that he had no money. Ireland was a poor country. In fact the crown on the King's head was worth more than the whole kingdom, and it was not a particularly valuable crown. His other three problems were his sons.

The King threw open the bedroom window and stuck out his head. The bird of the Golden Land stopped singing. She looked at this worried man with the heavy crown on. Then she spread her gold wings and flew away.

"Drat," said the King.

All the same, the next night the bird of the Golden Land came back. Again she perched on the window-sill and enchanted the King with her singing in his sleep. But in the morning she flew away as before as soon as she saw his face.

"Pickles," said the King. (He said "Pickles" not because he liked pickles but because he did not. "Pickles" was a favourite swear-word of his and he used it whenever he could.)

The following night the bird of the Golden Land did not come to sing to the King of Ireland in his sleep and he woke up more worried and unhappy than ever. Seven days and seven nights passed before the bird turned up again. Then it was in the afternoon, and the

King was in his counting house. He was in a terrible temper because he had nothing to count. The song of the bird soon soothed him, but by the time he had kicked aside all his empty treasure chests and rushed out into the garden to greet her—the bird was gone!

Now the King of Ireland fell into a very bad state of mind. He was too distressed even to swear. He could not eat and he could not drink. He hardly slept at all. All the time, whatever else he was doing, he was listening for something he thought he might never hear again . . . Because although there was this joy in his life—the beautiful song of the bird of the Golden Land—the King never knew when it might come to him, or even if it would come back at all. He lived for the song of the bird of the Golden Land. The song was the King's only pleasure, just as the crown was his only treasure. But while he could put the crown on his head whenever he liked, he could not command the song. To make matters worse, the more he stayed awake waiting for the bird, the less she seemed to visit him. And if he fell asleep then he could never be sure that he had not just wished to hear her and dreamt the whole thing. Finally the bird stopped coming altogether, and the King was ready to die of a broken heart.

It was at this point that the eldest son of the King of Ireland marched into the throne room and said:

"Father, I am old enough to marry."

"Go ahead," said the King.

"Well," said the eldest son, "I shall want some money to be married with."

"How much?" said the King.

"How much have you got?" said the eldest son.

The King spread his hands out wide and showed that there was nothing in them. The eldest son stared at the empty hands. Then he shook his head in disbelief and marched out. He was a tall fellow with red boots.

About noon on the same day, the second son of the King of Ireland marched into the throne room and said:

"Father, I am old enough to marry."

"It must be catching," said the King.

"Ha ha," said the second son. (He was not laughing. He said the words just like that: ha ha.) Then he said: "Well, I shall want some money to be married on."

"As much as your elder brother?" said the King.

"At least," said the second son. "How much is he getting?"

The King spread his hands out wide and showed that there was nothing in them. The second son stared at the empty hands. Then he shook his head in disbelief and marched out. He was a short fellow with black boots.

In the evening of the very same day, the King of Ireland was surprised to see his third and youngest son coming into the throne room. The King was surprised because although he knew things always go in threes he

7

had not expected his youngest son to be as bold or as greedy as the other two. The youngest son was the King of Ireland's favourite. He was less of a problem than the other two sons, although in a way he was more of a problem than the other two sons, because while they were a problem because they were bold and greedy he was a problem because he was a bit timid and lacking in ambition. His father loved him best of the three. This

third son of the King of Ireland was neither tall nor short, and he wore no boots. He had to go without because his brothers had bagged the first two pairs of boots made by the royal bootmaker, and the royal bootmaker refused to make a third pair seeing that the King could not afford to pay him for the first two. For this reason the third son of the King of Ireland was known as Prince Barefoot, although of course that was not his real name. By the way, he did not march into the throne room because it is difficult to march when you have nothing on your feet. Besides, marching was not his style. He walked in, smiling, with his hands in his pockets, and said:

"Hullo, Dad."

"Hullo, son," said the King.

"Dad . . ." said Prince Barefoot.

"Yes?" said the King.

"Dad, I don't quite know how to put this to you, but—"

The King sighed. "You think you're old enough to get married," he said.

"How did you guess?" demanded Prince Barefoot.

"Intuition," said the King. "Look," he went on, "I've no money. Ireland's broke."

"I'll do without money," said Prince Barefoot.

His father patted him on the shoulder. "Very good of you," he said. "But not so good for your wife."

Prince Barefoot shrugged. "I might marry someone who doesn't care any more about money than I do. You see, I don't have any particular wife in mind. I just wanted to know what you think of the idea in general."

"I approve of it," said the King. "Marriage is good for the temper. I used to be a much more agreeable fellow when your mother was alive. But you do need a bit of money to marry with." He took off his crown and looked at it while he scratched his head with his other

9

hand. "What's more," he went on, "your brothers have the same general idea in mind, and they have a keener sense than you of the business end of it."

The King of Ireland put his crown back on. He considered this youngest son standing so anxiously before him, shifting from one bare foot to the other as he waited for his father's verdict.

The King tipped his crown forward over his left temple at what he hoped was a jaunty angle. He winked his right eye. "Listen," he said. "Give me till tomorrow morning to think about a fair solution to all this."

When he went to bed that night the King of Ireland could not sleep. He had so little to give his sons, and it was impossible to work out a fair way of dividing what he did have. "Say I divide Ireland into two," he thought to himself, "and give one half to my eldest son and the other half to my second son. Then I could give the crown to my youngest son, Prince Barefoot. But if I give the crown to Barefoot the other two will be mad. The crown is worth more than the whole kingdom. There would be a war for the crown. And you can't cut a crown into halves or even thirds, because if you do it isn't a real crown any more. Oh what a dilemma! Oh what shall I do?"

At last, in the darkest hour that is always just before the dawn, the weary, worried King of Ireland fell asleep, his problems still unresolved. As he slept he dreamt a dream, and in his dream the bird of the Golden Land flew in at the window of the royal bedroom and perched on the crown that was resting on a plump little purple cushion by the side of the bed.

The bird fluffed up her gold feathers and began to sing. Her song inspired the King and he smiled in his sleep as he heard it. When he woke up the bird was gone. But his head was still full of her singing, and now he knew what he must do.

After breakfast the King of Ireland sent for his three

11

sons, and this is what he said to them:

"All three of you wish to marry. Very well. I approve. But it is hard for me to divide what I have among you, to give you each an equal start in life. If I give half of the kingdom to one of you, and the other half to another, and the crown to the third, that would not be fair. The trouble is that the crown is worth more than Ireland, and I cannot cut the crown in half or make parts of it for each of you. If I did that then none of you would ever be King, for a King must have a whole crown."

The eldest son, the prince in the red boots, could not stop yawning. He was bored by these explanations. The second son, the prince in the black boots, was picking his nose and not paying much attention. Prince Barefoot, on the other hand, nodded and looked sorry for his father.

The King of Ireland crossed to the window and stared out into the garden of his castle, which was all overgrown with weeds. "I have a plan," he said slowly. "There is a bird that comes to this castle and sings to me. I never know when she will come or when she will go. Her song is the sweetest thing I have ever heard in the world. They call her the bird of the Golden Land."

"The Golden Land doesn't exist," said his eldest son. "You must have imagined it."

"It's just a story to please children," said the second son. "There is no bird."

12

Prince Barefoot said nothing.

The King turned round and took off his crown and held it out before the three of them.

"Believe what you can," he said. "Nothing pleases me like the singing of that bird. There is a rare enchantment in her song. If I had her with me always I could live and die a happy man. So. I promise you this. Fetch me the bird of the Golden Land. The one who brings her to me will get the crown!"

Red Boots jumped up. "Well, there's no harm in trying," he said, "what with so much at stake."

Black Boots said: "Saddle my horse!"

As for Prince Barefoot, he said nothing, but he began making a bread and cheese sandwich, and then he wrapped it in a handkerchief to keep it fresh for eating on the quest.

The three brothers set forth. They travelled together until they came to a crossroads.

"I'm going right," said Red Boots.

"I'm going left," said Black Boots.

"It's getting dark," said Prince Barefoot. "Let's stay together until morning, and then go our separate ways."

The others laughed at him. They knew he was afraid of the dark. All the same, as they were laughing they saw the lamps being lit in a house on the hill above the crossroads, and since it was starting to rain quite heavily they decided to ask there for shelter for the night.

13

They knocked on the door and a woman answered it.

"Welcome, sons of the King of Ireland," she said. They went in.

"How do you know who we are?" demanded Red Boots.

"Oh, I know all about you," said the woman. "I know who you are. I know where you are going. And I know what you are looking for."

"Ha ha," said Black Boots, who was the sarcastic one. "Then you know that we are off on some fool's errand, looking for something that does not exist."

"You are looking for the bird of the Golden Land," said the woman.

"Do you know that bird?" asked Prince Barefoot. "Have you heard her song? Can you tell us the way to the Golden Land where she lives?"

The woman smiled and put her finger to her lips. Then she pointed to the corner of the room where an old man was asleep on a bed of dirty straw. "Wait until morning," she said. "My father will tell you what you must do. He is actually a devil, but he has his uses."

"That old beggar?" said Red Boots.

"Let's wake him now!" said Black Boots.

"If you do," said the woman, "he will turn into dust and you will never know anything."

Red Boots and Black Boots laughed at the very idea.

14

But Prince Barefoot drew his cloak about his ears and lay down on the floor and went to sleep, and after some arguing among themselves his two brothers thought better of waking the old man and they went to sleep also.

In the morning Prince Barefoot woke first and found the old man standing over him. The old man was very skinny. You could almost see his bones through his withered flesh. His eyes were like burning coals. Prince Barefoot was so scared that he nudged his two brothers and woke them straight away. There was no sign of the woman who had welcomed them to the house the night before. Indeed, there was no sign of the house. No walls, no lamps, no door, no room, no straw mattress, nothing. It seemed as though they had spent the night sleeping on the moorland.

"What's going on?" demanded Red Boots.

"Is this some hooky spooky devil's tricks?" said Black Boots.

The old man ignored their questions.

"You seek the bird of the Golden Land," he said. "Well, one of you may find her. But I can tell you—it's not easy!"

Red Boots looked down the hillside. At least the crossroads was still there in the valley below.

"Which way should we go then, grand-dad?" he asked craftily. "Left or right?"

"Neither left nor right," said the old man.

15

"Ha ha," said Black Boots. "But there are only two roads."

"The Golden Land is not reached by roads," the old man said. "Now, let the oldest and the strongest of you take that great sledge hammer which is lying over there. And let the second and most clever-clever take up the wicker basket beside it. And you, young man with no boots, who think you have no courage either, you take up the rope coiled beside the hammer and the basket. And then follow me, all three of you!"

The sons of the King of Ireland were impressed when they looked in the direction the old man was pointing his skinny finger—and saw a great sledge hammer, a big wicker basket, and a thick coil of rope, just as he had described. Red Boots took the hammer. Black Boots put the wicker basket on his back. And Prince Barefoot picked up the coil of rope and looped it round his arm.

The old man strode off down the hillside towards the crossroads. He moved with surprising speed for one so ancient. When he reached the crossroads he cackled with laughter.

"Left goes nowhere," he said.

"Right goes everywhere," he said.

"Neither nowhere nor everywhere leads to the Golden Land," he added.

Then he stabbed with his finger at a tall rock standing upright precisely where the roads were joined together.

16

"Now," he cried to the eldest son of the King of Ireland. "Hit that rock as hard as you can!"

Red Boots shrugged. He swung the hammer. He hit the rock with all his might.

The rock split down the middle and the two halves fell to the ground.

There was a gaping hole beneath it.

The old man grinned at the three sons of the King of Ireland. "Now then, my lads," he said, "that is the one and only way to the Golden Land. We are standing, you see, in the middle of Ireland. There used to be a little narrow hole in that rock which was just big enough for the bird of the Golden Land to fly up and fly down. But now there is a big hole, isn't there? Big enough for the King's sons, would you say?"

17

Red Boots got down on his knees and peered over the edge of the hole.

"Are you sure, grand-dad?" he demanded.

"Isn't this another hooky spooky devil's trick?" said Black Boots, peering too.

"It's certainly deep enough," said Prince Barefoot, his knees beginning to knock together. "I can't see to the bottom of it."

"Whichever one of you is the bravest," the old man said, "can go down that hole in the wicker basket. If he has luck he will get to the bottom safely."

"And if he hasn't?" said Prince Barefoot, his teeth chattering.

"If he hasn't then he'll be killed when the wicker basket hits the rocks on the way," said the old man. "You must tie the rope to the basket, you see, and let it down. And as it goes down it will swing from side to side."

Red Boots was fastening the rope to the wicker basket.

"I will go down," he said. "What is at the bottom of the hole?"

"At the bottom of the hole," said the old man, "is the straight road which you must follow if you are ever to win the bird of the Golden Land."

Black Boots and Prince Barefoot held the rope steady and lowered the wicker basket down the hole with their eldest brother in it. But as the basket got further down it began to sway from side to side like a pendulum, and to hit against the rocks.

"Pull me up again!" cried Red Boots. He was convinced that it was all nonsense anyway, and that the old man was simply trying to kill them.

So Black Boots and Prince Barefoot pulled hard on the rope and brought their brother back up to the world again.

"There's nothing down there," said Red Boots, dusting his clothes and pretending that he had not been scared.

"Ha ha," said Black Boots. "Then I will try!"

So Black Boots got into the wicker basket and Red Boots and Prince Barefoot held the rope steady and lowered him down the hole. However, he did not get even as far as Red Boots had got before he started screaming and hollering to be pulled up again. When he came back out of the hole his face was white with fright and he did not even say anything sarcastic.

"What about you?" said the old man to Prince Barefoot.

Poor Barefoot! He was so nervous that he could not speak. Cruelly, his brothers pretended that his silence meant that he was willing. They picked him up, each of them holding him under one shoulder, and they pushed him into the wicker basket. Then, before he could let out a squeak of protest, they started lowering the basket down the hole. They did not care for him,

19

and they were not gentle in the way they did the lowering. The basket went down the hole at a great speed, but this was actually to Barefoot's advantage because it meant that it went down in a straight line and hardly bumped against the sides at all. Before he could shout back up the hole for them to pull him out again, the basket reached the bottom with a thump!

Prince Barefoot was dazed by the thump but not hurt. He tumbled out of the basket, bruising his shins and elbows but breaking no bones. In the panic of the fall down the hole, he had shut his eyes tight. Now he opened them. He was astonished to find that he had to keep blinking because he had arrived in a place of great light and brightness.

Under his feet was a road of gold.

Moving first one bare foot and then the other, Prince Barefoot began to walk slowly forward along the road of gold. It felt warm under the soles of his feet. It was a very straight road, and it stretched into the distance for as far as he could see in this strange underground country of unbelievable brilliance. There were gold trees along the sides of the road and gold rivers under bridges of solid gold. The light seemed to come out of all these golden things. Once Barefoot's eyes grew used to it, he found it a pleasant place to be.

Barefoot walked and walked. At last he came to the end of the long straight road paved with gold. There, built right across the road so that the road ran in at its front door, was a fine castle. This castle was made of solid gold also.

Prince Barefoot knocked on the door and a woman answered it.

"Welcome, son of the King of Ireland," she said.

They went in.

"How do you know who I am?" asked Barefoot.

"Oh, I know all about you," said the woman. "I know who you are. I know where you are going. And I know what you are looking for."

"The bird," said Barefoot eagerly. "The bird of the Golden Land."

21

"Of course," said the woman.

"Well, where is she?" asked Barefoot, looking round. But the walls of the castle inside were of polished gold and all he could see was himself and the woman reflected in their shining surfaces.

The woman tossed back her golden hair and laughed merrily. "Listen, little Prince No-Boots," she said in a kind voice, "I will give you all the help and advice I can. But to find and catch the bird of the Golden Land is not easy. You have come down the long black hole, right?"

"Yes," said Barefoot, shuddering at the memory.

"That was brave," said the woman. "And you have walked for miles and miles along the long straight road, right?"

"I have," said Barefoot.

"Well, all that is good," the woman said. "But now the harder tasks begin. The road that runs in at the front door of this castle is straight and not complicated, as you know. But the road that runs out at the back door is a road that is so twisty you would take seven years to get to the end of it and seven years to come back here again. It loops like a snake, you see, that road out the back, and for every seven miles it goes forward it goes six miles back. What's worse, it isn't really a road when you get to the hardest bit."

"I think I'll go home then," Barefoot said.

"You are free to do just as you please," said the

22

woman. "But I told you I would help you and I will. It would take you seven years to *walk* to the end of that road and seven years to come back. But you could *ride* there, and do what you must do, and be back here again in a year and a day. That is, if you know how to ride a horse?"

Now Barefoot knew how to ride a horse and the woman's words rather hurt his pride. So he answered:

"All princes can ride."

"Quite so," said the woman. "But there is one horse that only one prince can ride. Follow me!"

She led him to the stable at the back of the castle. It was full of beautiful horses. All the horses had gold coats and gold manes and their eyes were like golden stones that blazed.

"Take your pick," said the woman, standing back.

Barefoot was terrified. He gazed from one horse to another. "All these horses are too tall and strong for me," he thought to himself. "If I fall from any one of them the fall will kill me."

Then behind the stable door he saw another horse. It was a poor little mare. This mare was gold in colour too, but her coat was shaggy and her mane was clotted with mud and you could see her ribs under her flanks. "At least if I fall off that one," thought Barefoot, "I won't have far to fall."

So he combed the little mare, and cleaned her, and saddled and bridled her with a little gold saddle and

23

bridle he found hanging on a golden hook, and then he led her out of the stable by the back door.

The woman was waiting for him.

"I see," she said, when she saw the mare.

"I'm sorry," said Barefoot, putting one bare foot into the stirrup and mounting. "I'm not much—"

The woman touched her finger to her lips to hush him.

" I see," she went on, "that you might be the right prince. For you have chosen the right horse."

Barefoot's eyes opened wide. "The smallest horse in the stable?" he said.

"The swiftest horse in all the Golden Land!" said the woman.

And so saying she touched the little mare lightly on

24

the withers and the mare sped forward down the twisty
gold road. She galloped so fast that Prince Barefoot
could not see where they were going. It was all a golden
blur. And to make matters worse the road must have
been as bad as the woman had warned him it would be,
for they were twisting and turning at every stride. Poor
Barefoot began to feel quite sick, but he held on tight to
the mane of the little gold mare, and kept his eyes shut
and hoped for the best.

When they had been going for three months the
mare spoke and said:

"King's son, open your eyes."

Prince Barefoot opened his eyes.

"Tell me what you see," instructed the mare.

"What do I see?" said Barefoot, winking and

blinking and shaking his head. "Why, I can't see anything for shining. It's all too bright. And besides we're going too fast!"

"Then look between my two ears," said the mare.

Barefoot crouched low along the mare's neck and looked between her ears. All at once his vision cleared. He saw a sea ahead of them. It was a cruel sea, with great gold waves in it and gold foam blowing in the wind like a terrible fog.

Prince Barefoot tugged on the reins.

"Whee! Stop!" he cried. "I see a terrible ocean. We'll be drowned!"

In Ireland to this day, by the way, the word that will stop a horse is *whee* not *whoa*, and Barefoot thought it would be the same in the Golden Land.

But the little gold mare did not stop.

"Whee! Whee!" shouted Barefoot, pulling at the reins with all his might.

The mare just whinneyed and shook her head and galloped the faster.

"This," she said, "is where we start to find out if you are really the right King's son, and the one who will win the bird of the Golden Land."

And without another word she galloped straight into the sea. The waves were enormous. The water crashed about horse and rider. Barefoot had his eyes shut tight. But after a while, as he realised he was not sinking or drowning, he opened one eye and saw that the mare

26

was now running on top of the sea just as though it were solid land. "This is witchcraft!" thought Barefoot, and again he was so scared that he lost his grip on the mane of the little mare, and slid down her back although he did not fall off. Then he opened his other eye and saw that they were nearing the other side of the sea.

"Where are you now?" said the horse as they galloped up out of the sea and onto the twisty gold road again.

"I'm sitting near your tail," Prince Barefoot gasped. "I'm almost falling!"

The mare said only:

"Don't fall. Be brave. The right prince will ride me right."

They travelled on.

When they had been going for another three months the little gold mare spoke again and said:

"King's son, are your eyes open?"

"One of them is," said Barefoot.

"Good," said the horse. "You are getting braver. Now open your other eye and look between my two ears and tell me what you see."

Barefoot clutched onto the gold mane and pulled himself right up the horse's neck. He looked forward between her pricked ears.

He shuddered.

"I see a second ocean," he cried. "It's worse than the first!"

It was worse too. Its waves were like towers falling.

27

The spray off the waves was like gold bricks being thrown about by a giant.

"Whee!" shouted Barefoot.

But the mare did not stop.

"This," she said, "is where we go on finding out if you are really the right King's son, and the one who will win the bird of the Golden Land."

They galloped across the second sea. Although it was worse than the first, Prince Barefoot found that this time he was not quite so scared. All the same, he kept crouched flat against the little mare's neck, with his arms about it.

"Where are you now?" said the horse as they galloped up out of the second sea and onto the twisty gold road again.

"I'm out at your ears," admitted Barefoot. "I'm almost falling!"

But the mare said only:

"Don't fall. You're getting braver every time. And the right prince will ride me right."

They travelled on, faster than ever.

When they had been going for another three months the little gold mare spoke again and said:

"King's son, are your eyes open?"

"They are," said Prince Barefoot.

"Both of them?" said the horse.

"Both of them," said Prince Barefoot boldly. "And you don't need to tell me to look between your two ears

28

and say what I can see. I *am* looking. And I can already see a third ocean. It's by far the worst of the lot, and by far the broadest. But a daresay we'll get across, won't we?''

"We might," said the mare. "I cannot guarantee it. If you are really the right King's son, and the one who will win the bird of the Golden Land, then we may cross this sea as well as we crossed the others, though not so easily. If you are not the right prince there is no escape for us!''

Prince Barefoot patted his horse's neck as she started to gallop over the third and most terrible gold ocean, where the waves were like thunder and lightning or planets crashing together. He had grown fond of this little mare who had served him so well up to now.

"What about *you*?'' he managed to cry in her ear. "It's not fair that *you* should drown if I am the wrong prince.''

"Thank you," said the mare. "You don't have to worry about me, but I'm glad that you do.''

She galloped on over the water. Her breathing was getting very harsh and laboured. Prince Barefoot wanted to slow her down.

"It's all right," gasped the mare. "We have to go fast or we sink. That's the only way to run on gold water.'' She took a deep breath as she kept the pace up. "Three islands," she panted.

"Three islands?'' repeated Prince Barefoot, not

understanding. But he did understand when the mare ran on without slackening speed until they reached a tiny gold island sticking up out of the sea. The island was no bigger than a rock, but it was big enough for the horse to stand on, blowing and sweating, until she got her wind back. Then she sped on again over the dreadful sea until they came to a second island, as small as the first, but big enough for her to stand on and rest as before. There was a third island where she could rest for a last time before making it safely to the far shore of that ultimate ocean.

"Where are you now?" said the mare as they resumed their way on the twisty gold road.

Prince Barefoot replied:

"I am sitting on the saddle in the middle of your back."

And the mare said quietly:

"That is where the right prince would be who rode me right."

They went on now for only a few hours without adventure. Then Prince Barefoot saw in the distance a great and shining palace of solid gold.

"I wonder who lives in that palace," he said aloud.

Then the little gold mare spoke and said:

"That is the palace of the King of the Golden Land."

Prince Barefoot nodded. "I thought it must be," he admitted. "I've never seen anything half as splendid."

"The palace is nothing," said the mare. "The palace

31

is glorified dust. It is what is *in* the palace that is the true miracle you seek."

Prince Barefoot whispered:

"Do you mean the bird of the Golden Land?"

The little mare jingled her bridle and ignored the question. "Listen, little Prince No-Boots," she said in a kind voice, "and I will tell you what to do. Behind that shining palace are thirteen stables. At the first stable we come to thirteen stable boys will run out to take me from you, saying that they will comb me and clean me and care for me. You must take no notice of them. You must drive them away, and tell them that you will take care of your own horse. Ride on. At the second stable it will be the same, only this time there will be only twelve stable boys. Refuse them too. Ride on. And so on, and so on, until you have left twelve stables behind you. Dismount at the thirteenth stable, and lead me in."

"And who will be the single stable boy in the thirteenth stable?" asked Prince Barefoot.

"A good question," said the little gold mare. But she did not answer it.

Prince Barefoot approached the shining palace. He rode the mare past the first stable. At once, just as the horse had foretold, thirteen stable boys came running out and tried to seize the bridle.

"Stand aside," Prince Barefoot commanded them. "I take care of my own horse."

It was the same at each succeeding stable. First

32

twelve, then eleven, then ten, then nine, then eight, then seven, then six, then five, then four, then three, then two stable boys all tried to take the little gold mare, claiming that they would comb her and clean her and care for her. But at each attempt the youngest son of the King of Ireland made the same reply:

"Stand aside! I take care of my own horse!"

When the horse and rider reached the thirteenth stable there was no sign of a stable boy. However, the straw in this thirteenth stable was of the cleanest gold, and the oats in the manger looked like grains of gold dust—only they must have been a good deal more tasty than gold dust because when Prince Barefoot had removed his mount's saddle and bridle and reins and bit the little mare stuck her head in the manger and nuzzled away contentedly. Barefoot drew water for her too, from a golden pump into a golden bucket, and the mare drank until she had had her fill.

At this moment the stable boy for the thirteenth stable appeared from behind a bale of golden hay. Prince Barefoot saw at a glance that he was not really a stable boy at all. For a start he had a crown on his head. And for a second and third thing he was holding a golden sceptre in his right hand and a golden orb in his left.

Prince Barefoot bowed politely.

"Good day to you, King of the Golden Land," he said.

"Good rubbish," said the King of the Golden Land. "And who might you be, Master Bootless?"

"I am the youngest son of the King of Ireland," said Prince Barefoot with as much dignity as he could muster.

"You are the youngest son of a drunken tinker," said the King of the Golden Land. "How dare you go riding past all my finest stables? Aren't my stable boys good enough for you and your flea-bitten nag of a horse? Besides, what's a barefoot brat like you doing here in my palace in the first place?"

Barefoot did not lose his temper. "I meant no insult to your stable boys," he explained. "I prefer to take care of my own horse, that's all. Surely, the great King of the Golden Land is not going to deny me the use of his smallest and simplest stable, or the pleasure of caring for the horse that brought me here over such a long road?"

The King of the Golden Land had narrow gold eyes, like slits with congealed honey behind them. Only the honey did not look sweet. In fact it looked like a golden poison.

"Your fine words don't fool me," he sneered. "I know why you've come here. You're in search of the bird of the Golden Land."

"I am," admitted Prince Barefoot.

The King of the Golden Land smiled nastily. He had gold teeth as sharp as any shark's.

34

"Those who come in search of the miraculous have to go through hell," he said.

"What do you mean?" asked Prince Barefoot.

"You'll find out soon enough," promised the King of the Golden Land. He rubbed his hands together and Barefoot noticed that a thin gold dust flaked from them as he rubbed. "You have to work for your reward," the King went on. "You have to pass tests. You have to prove that you are the right prince. And even then you might not win the bird."

The King turned aside and spat. Prince Barefoot noticed that his spit was a golden guinea that rolled on the ground before disappearing down a mouse hole.

"I'm sick of all you King's sons coming down here so bold to try your luck and win my bird," said the King of the Golden Land.

"I'm not especially bold," said Barefoot.

The King's eyes got even narrower. He stared at the young man standing before him. Those thin gold eyes travelled slowly and critically down from the fresh and innocent face to the feet that did not even have the cheapest boots to protect them.

"Yes," he said slowly. "I can see that you're not especially anything, Master Bootless."

Barefoot stared at his dusty feet.

The mare snorted as she stirred in the stall behind him.

"Come with me to my palace," said the King.

35

Prince Barefoot followed the King of the Golden
Land into his shining palace. It was full of gold
furniture and gold curtains and all the floors were of
gold inlaid with rubies and pearls and other precious
stones that winked in the light of the golden
chandeliers. They sat down at a golden-topped table in
a golden hall and they ate golden perch and golden
apples and golden eagles seasoned with golden herbs,
all off platters of beaten gold. There was also a kind of
liquid gold to drink from golden goblets, but Barefoot
found this too sweet and sickly for his taste and did not
finish it.

When the meal was over, the King raised his goblet
in a mocking toast:

"Here's to your downfall, Bootless!"

Prince Barefoot responded without losing his temper:

36

"To the health of the King of the Golden Land!"

The King wiped his mouth with the back of his hand, leaving a sticky gold smear across his knuckles.

He leaned forwards across the golden-topped table.

"The real tests begin tomorrow," he said.

His face was so wicked in the gold light of the candles that Barefoot would have been shaking in his shoes—if he had had any shoes to shake in.

"What tests?" he said.

The King held up a glass of golden water and grinned at him through it.

"Tomorrow," he announced, smacking his lips. "Tomorrow at sunrise I will hide. I will disappear. I will vanish. And you, Master Bootless, will have just until sunset to find me."

"And if I cannot find you?"

"If you cannot find me," said the King of the Golden Land, "you will lose your head. Like this! Chop!"

And he sliced the top off a golden egg with a knife of solid gold, so that all the golden yolk ran everywhere.

Prince Barefoot was shown to a bedchamber in the palace, but he could not sleep there. All the shadows in the room seemed gold and stalking and behaved like murderers creeping up on him every time he felt like nodding off. At last he could stand it no longer. He slid out from between the silky golden sheets and crept down to the stable where the little mare was tethered. He told her the whole story.

37

"What am I to do?" he said. "The King will hide. I will never find him. He will cut off my head!"

The mare considered him kindly with her soft gold eyes. "That is all tomorrow," she said. "Sleep now. You're worn out."

"But I can't sleep," protested Barefoot. "I'm far too worried to sleep a wink."

The mare lifted her right foreleg.

"Lie down there beneath the manger," she instructed him.

Prince Barefoot was so tired that he did what she said without question. Then the mare gave him a gentle tap with her right hoof. He was asleep in an instant and slept all night a deep and dreamless sleep until in the morning the mare gave him another gentle tap, this time with her left hoof, and he woke up again.

Just for a moment Barefoot lay warm and snug in the golden straw, gazing up at the horse which had proved such a good friend to him. Then he remembered the task ahead.

"The sun has risen," he said. 'Where shall I find the King?"

"No trouble," replied the mare. "Walk into the palace garden. You will find that it's full of beautiful maidens. Each one of them will praise you, or show you some unusual flower, or ask you to walk with her and talk with her and gaze into her eyes. Pay no attention to them! Not one! Don't even look at their faces, or the faces of the flowers they try to show you. Instead, you must walk straight to the middle of the garden where there is a tall tree growing. On the topmost branch of the tree there's a single gold apple. Pluck that apple! Cut it in half! The King will come out!"

Prince Barefoot did everything just as the mare had commanded. He walked in the palace garden. It was full of beautiful maidens, and every maiden in the garden kept teasing him to walk with her or talk with her or gaze into her eyes. They praised him also, as they walked beside him, and tried to engage his attention by showing him unusual flowers which they picked from the borders.

But Barefoot did not look at the maidens or the flowers.

He kept walking straight, with his eyes fixed fast on his own bare feet.

When we reached the middle of the garden he looked up and saw the tall tree growing. High up, on the topmost branch of the tree, was the single gold apple.

Barefoot was a good climber and he made the most use of his climbing skills now. In no time at all, he had reached the topmost branch of the tall tree in the middle of the palace garden, and plucked the gold apple, and slid down the trunk again to stand on the ground with the apple clutched tight in his hand.

The most beautiful of the maidens in the palace

garden was waiting for him. She was the daughter of the King of the Golden Land. When she saw what he held in his hand, she said:

"Tell me, little prince who shins up trees like a monkey on a stick, what do you intend to do with the gold apple?"

Prince Barefoot rubbed the apple against his sleeve. "Why, this is the most remarkable apple I've ever seen in my life," he said. "I intend to take it back with me to Ireland, that's what."

"Oh no you don't," said the daughter of the King of the Golden Land. "That apple belongs to my father, and you're not taking it anywhere."

Barefoot put his head on one side and pretended to consider the rights and wrongs of the situation.

"All right," he said at last. "I'll tell you what I'll do, for your sake, since you ask me."

"What?" said the King's daughter, thinking that she had outwitted him.

"I'll only take half," said Prince Barefoot. "And I'll leave you the rest."

So saying, he drew out his dagger and made halves of the apple, and out jumped the King of the Golden Land.

"Oh, oh, oh, oh," the King cried loudly. "That's one cut in my head today!"

Prince Barefoot bowed. "I'm sorry," he said. "But how was I to know that a great and mighty monarch

like yourself would be hiding in an apple?"

They went back into the shining palace and ate another disgusting golden dinner. Then the King said:

"I will hide again in the morning. Find me before sunset or I'll have your head for a football."

Prince Barefoot did not even try to sleep in the royal bedchamber. Instead he crept down to the smallest stable where the little gold mare was tethered and told her all that had happened.

41

"Don't fret," said the mare.

"Lie down there beneath the manger," she added.

Prince Barefoot did as he was told. The mare gave him another gentle tap with her right hoof. Barefoot was asleep in a trice and slept all night a deep and dreamless sleep until in the morning the loyal horse gave him a tap with her left hoof and he woke up refreshed.

"The sun's up," Barefoot said. "Where shall I find the King today?"

"No trouble," replied the mare. "Walk straight from this stable and into the palace kitchen. A great many beautiful maidens will be there before you. Some of them will laugh at you. Some of them will tease you and push you and slap you with towels. But never even look at them or mind them, my little Prince No-Boots. Just walk up to the fire. The cook will give you a bowl of hot soup without a spoon in it. Then you say, 'Look here, cook, I must have a spoon.' Walk across to the cupboard. In a drawer in the cupboard you will find a gold spoon. Take the spoon and snap it in half. The King will come out!"

The youngest son of the King of Ireland did just as the little gold mare had commanded. He went to the kitchen. He avoided the chattering and the teasing of the maidens. He took the bowl of hot soup from the cook by the fire, saying 'But I must have a spoon for my soup.' Then he crossed to the cupboard, and opened

42

the top drawer, and took out the gold spoon that was in it.

The daughter of the King of the Golden Land was watching his every movement carefully. When she saw the gold spoon in his hand, she said:

"Tell me, little prince who runs about in kitchens like a pot boy, what do you intend to do with that gold spoon?"

Prince Barefoot breathed on the spoon and then rubbed it bright with his thumb and smiled at his reflection in it. "Why, this is the most remarkable spoon I've ever seen in my life," he said. "I intend to take it back with me to Ireland, that's what."

The daughter of the King of the Golden Land shook her head crossly. "Oh no you don't," she snapped, trying to snatch the spoon from him without success. "That spoon belongs to my father, and you're not taking it anywhere."

Barefoot put his head on one side and pretended to consider the rights and wrongs of the situation.

"All right," he said at last. "I don't want to be a thief. I'll tell you what I'll do then, since you ask me."

"What?" said the King's daughter, half expecting another trick.

She was right to expect a trick.

Prince Barefoot pushed the end of the spoon back into the drawer, then he slammed the drawer shut and banged down on the bowl of the spoon with all his might. The spoon broke into neat halves and out jumped the King of the Golden Land.

"Oh, oh, oh, oh," the King cried loudly. "I've two cuts in my head now. One yesterday, one today."

Prince Barefoot bowed low. "I apologise, of course," he said. "How was I to know that a great and mighty monarch like yourself would be skulking in a spoon?"

That evening in the shining palace the King of the Golden Land and the youngest son of the King of Ireland ate another nauseating dinner of gold meats and fishes served on golden platters. When they had finished the King gave a gilt-edged burp and said:

"I will hide again tomorrow, you know. And the third time is always the hardest. You must find me before sunset or I'll give your head to my daughter for a pin cushion."

Prince Barefoot waited until everyone in the palace was asleep and then he crept down again to the stable where his faithful little mare was waiting. She put him to sleep as before, with a tap of her right hoof, and he slept peacefully until the usual tap with the left hoof in the morning.

"Where shall I find the King today?" asked Barefoot as soon as he woke up.

"It will be harder work today," the mare confessed, "but you will find him. Take some grains of barley and go to that pond near the palace garden. You will see a gold duck swimming around by herself in the water.

44

Throw the barley on the bank, and the duck will come to get it. While she is picking and pecking at the grains you must catch her, and hold her in your hands, and tell her to lay an egg. She will refuse. Say then that if she doesn't lay an egg you will kill her with your bare hands about her neck. The duck will lay an egg then. And the King of the Golden Land will be in that egg!"

Prince Barefoot did as the little gold mare had told him. He took some barley and he went down to the pond near the palace garden. He threw the barley on the bank. He caught the duck. And he told the duck to lay an egg.

"How can I lay an egg when I don't have one to lay?" the duck demanded.

"Well, I'll kill you if you don't," Prince Barefoot said.

The duck quacked. She laid the egg. It was the

goldest egg the world had ever seen, and for that matter, golder than anything ever seen in the underworld of the Golden Land either.

The daughter of the King of the Golden Land had been hiding in the bushes beside the pond. When she saw the duck's egg in Prince Barefoot's hand, she said:

"Tell me, little prince who bullies ducks, what do you intend to do with that golden egg?"

Barefoot tossed the duck's egg up and down in his hand. He smiled. "Well," he said, "I'm not intending to take it back with me to Ireland."

"Oh," said the King's daughter, a bit surprised. "That's good news, at any rate."

"No," explained Barefoot, "it would go bad before I got home. So I think I'll just eat it here and now!"

"You can't!" cried the King's daughter. "You can't! You musn't! That's my father's egg, it belongs to him!"

"I see," said Barefoot, his head on one side, considering. "I'll be fair about it then. I'll give you half of it!"

And so saying he split the golden egg in two, and of course out jumped the King of the Golden Land with his face and beard all runny with egg yolk.

"Oh, oh, oh, oh," the King cried loudly. "That's three cuts in my head now. One yesterday, one the day before, and the worst of the lot today!"

Prince Barefoot made such a deep bow that his forehead touched the ground. "How sorry I am," he said. "I do hope you will forgive me? But, really, how was I to know that a great and mighty monarch like yourself would be hatching in an egg?"

The King of the Golden Land was so angry that it looked as though his thin little eyes would explode and golden tears burst out like lava from an erupting volcano. He stamped his goldshod foot and made a golden hole in the ground. Then he twisted his gingerbread coloured beard for a bit, wringing the egg yolk from it, until he had calmed down.

"Very well," he said. "Very golden well." Those gilt eyes glinted. "You have beaten me, Master Bootless, so it seems . . ."

"And the bird of the Golden Land?" said Barefoot. "Is she mine then?"

The King laughed long and loud, showing his bright shark's teeth. "Not yet," he sneered. "Not ever, probably. You see, *you* have found *me* three times, but the tests are not finished yet. Oh no, not by a long golden chalk! For now it is *your* turn to hide. Tomorrow I shall come looking for you from sunrise until sunset. And the day after that the same. And the day after that also." The King rubbed his hands together so hard that the gold dust flew from them like sparks or shavings from a saw. "And on the first day that I find you, little goody No-Boots," he promised, "I will have your head and stick it on a spike on the topmost tower of my splendid shining palace. You came down here to get

47

the bird of the Golden Land? Well, I'll tell you—it's more likely that the crows and the kites and the vultures of the Golden Land are going to get *you*!"

Poor Barefoot did not feel like another wretched golden dinner in the King's banqueting hall. Instead, he went for a walk round the palace garden, kicking at the golden pebbles and thinking over his predicament. He sat down on a bench and felt sorry for himself. Then he began to feel hungry, and remembering the bread and cheese sandwich he had prepared for himself so long ago when first setting out on this journey to the underworld he unwrapped the handkerchief in which he had put it. The sandwich was a bit over nine months old, but to Barefoot it tasted like manna from heaven. It was at least real food, he reflected, and not just edible gold.

When he had finished the bread and cheese sandwich, and tossed the remaining crumbs to the duck that had laid the golden egg for him, Prince Barefoot made his way through the misty gold twilight and down to the stable where his trusty mare was tethered.

"You look more miserable than ever," the mare observed, glancing up from her oats.

"I am more miserable than ever," said Barefoot. "Oh little gold mare, my only friend, it's all up for me now! I'm in deep deep trouble this time, and there's no getting out!"

"How's that?" asked the horse.

"The King of the Golden Land has told me I must hide," said Barefoot. "And the first day of three that he catches me he will kill me and cut off my head."

"No trouble," said the horse.

"No trouble!" cried Prince Barefoot. "Look, it's all right for him. He's magic. He can hide in anything he likes, and I only find him because you tell me where he is. But I'm not magic, am I? I'm just an ordinary run-of-the-mill King's son without even a pair of decent boots to his name. How can I hope to hide so that he doesn't find me and have my head to decorate the top of his palace?"

The little gold mare gave a snort so that husks and oats flew out of the manger.

"Go to sleep, my Prince No-Boots," she advised him. "It will all come out right, just you wait and see."

And the horse put Barefoot to sleep as before, with a tap of her right hoof, and he did not even have a dream to disturb his rest before morning, when she woke him again with her left hoof's gentle tap.

"Where am I going to hide?" whispered Barefoot immediately.

The sun was beginning to rise and the King was coming. Barefoot could hear the marching boots of his men in the stable yard.

The little gold mare rolled her eyes. Then she flicked the youngest son of the King of Ireland with her golden tail and nickered:

"*He! He! Go into a flea!*"

All at once Prince Barefoot found himself turned into
a flea on the floor of the stable. He leapt and he jumped
and enjoyed himself hopping about all day until
darkfall. Meanwhile, the King of the Golden Land
gnashed his shark's teeth and tugged and twisted at his
gingerbread moustaches while his stable boys searched
high and low in the stable.

When the King returned, baffled, to his shining
palace, the mare made a man again of Prince Barefoot,
and said to him:

"The King of the Golden Land will ask you where
you were hiding. Don't tell him. Just say that you
didn't ask *him* such a question the day he was hiding in
an apple in his garden."

So Barefoot went to the palace.

"You beat me today," said the King. "Where were
you hiding? What form were you in?"

Barefoot shook his head.

"I didn't ask you such a question the day you were in the apple," he replied.

The King scowled. His hairy golden eyebrows met over his gold slit eyes.

"Just wait until tomorrow, Master Bootless!"

The next morning, when the mare roused the youngest son of the King of Ireland with a tap of her left hoof, she flicked him with her golden tail and nickered:

"He! He! Go into a bee!"

The King of the Golden Land turned all the thirteen stables upside down looking for Prince Barefoot, but he did not find him. Barefoot, for his part, disguised as a bee, was buzzing about and gathering honey most of the morning, and in the afternoon he ate it. It was altogether a most agreeable day for him.

In the evening the mare made Barefoot a man again, and he went to the palace in his proper shape.

"Clever stuff," said the King. "Give us a clue!

51

Where were you hiding? What form were you in?"

"Come now, your majesty," said Barefoot reprovingly. "I didn't ask you such a question the day you were in the spoon."

The King of the Golden Land said nothing. He spat in the fire instead, and the spit went off like a banger on Guy Fawkes' Night.

"Tomorrow!" he barked.

But tomorrow was no use to him either. When Prince Barefoot was woken up by the gentle tap of the mare's left hoof, and had been flicked by her golden tail, she nickered:

"Beware! Beware! Go into a hair!"

And this time Barefoot was turned into one of the golden hairs in the little mare's eyelashes, so that although the King combed and brushed the horse and inspected every likely part of her as well as every nook and cranny in the thirteen stables he could not find what he was looking for.

As night fell the King of the Golden Land returned to his palace empty-handed. He was frothing at the mouth with rage. The froth, of course, was molten gold. Marigolds sprang up out of the ground where it fell, so that was at least some good.

The mare turned Barefoot back into a man again. Then she nuzzled her nose against his shoulder and said:

"Now, little Prince No-Boots, here is the hardest

52

part. You must go to the palace. The King will be raging. There is only one thing that will calm him and please him—and that is the song of the bird of the Golden Land."

"Where is that bird?" cried Prince Barefoot. "Are you sure she exists? Not a sound of her song have I heard since I came down here."

The mare shook her head in disgust.

"Mankind!" she snorted.

"What do you mean?" asked Barefoot.

"I mean that you haven't been listening," said the mare. "Who do you think it was whose voice sang to me in the night when you were asleep, telling me all the things you had to do to outwit the King?"

Prince Barefoot shrugged. "Then she wants to escape to the world above? She wants me to save her?"

"Perhaps," said the little mare. "The love of a true prince might keep her above in the world. Who knows? But, remember, even if you win her it will always be in her power to be the bird of the Golden Land as well as the Queen with the Three Crowns."

"The Queen with the Three Crowns?" said Barefoot. "I don't understand."

"Never mind understanding," the horse advised him. "Go to the shining palace. Placate the King. Don't say a word to annoy him. That bird of the Golden Land no longer belongs to him. She comes and she goes as she pleases. But if you sing to the King and tell him stories

53

and poems then it is possible that the bird will fly in at the window, for she loves nothing more than to sing and hear poetry said. If the bird of the Golden Land comes in at the window and is pleased by your songs and your stories and poems then she will sing also. She does not always sing for sorrow. And her singing for joy or for sorrow will assuredly lull the King of the Golden Land to sleep. He sleeps only once in seven years, by the way, and that when the bird is there to sing to him. Now, as soon as the King is asleep, all his men will fall asleep with him. Then you must take up the bird of the Golden Land in your own bare hands, and put her gently in the golden cage that hangs by the King's bedside, and run with her on tiptoe to the front door of the palace. I shall be waiting for you there. Good luck! God speed!"

The youngest son of the King of Ireland was a careful fellow. When you go through life with no boots you learn to take care. Now he went to the palace and carried out every instruction the little gold mare had given him. He placated the King of the Golden Land. He said not a single word to annoy him. He sang to the King and told him all the best stories and poems he had ever heard in his life. Ireland is a great country for songs and for poems and stories, so the King of the Golden Land was soon well pleased by this night's entertainment. He stretched out his feet to the golden blaze of the fire and clasped his hands behind his head

54

and listened attentively to everything Barefoot had to sing or say.

After a while, just as the clock struck midnight, both Barefoot and the King of the Golden Land became aware that something or someone else was listening too.

There was a beating of wings at the window.

The golden candles bent and bowed.

And the bird of the Golden Land flew in!

Prince Barefoot could hardly believe his eyes. He had never seen anything so beautiful. The eyes of the bird were green and her feathers were gold. She sang as she flew. Prince Barefoot could hardly believe his ears either. The song was so magical. He had never heard anything like it. It was a sad sweetness. It was a laughing sigh. It was a hymn of joy with tears in it. It made you glad to be alive and not at all scared to die. Heaven, thought Barefoot, would be made of songs like this.

If any such thoughts were passing through the head of the King of the Golden Land then his face gave no sign of them. All the same, a gross grin of contentment spread across his fat features. He sucked with his shark's teeth at his gingerbread moustache. He took off his boots. He started to snore. His head fell back among the gold-embroidered cushions. He was asleep.

In the same instant that the King of the Golden Land fell asleep, all the King's men fell asleep also.

Some of them went to sleep leaning on their golden spears. Some of them just slid down and curled up in golden knots on the floor. One of them fell forwards and slept with his face turned half sideways in a bowl of golden lentil soup, blowing bubbles as he slept.

Prince Barefoot stood up.

He tiptoed towards the bird of the Golden Land.

With infinite gentleness he cradled her in his bare hands and placed her, still singing, in the golden cage that was hanging by the King's bedside.

The bird looked at him with her eyes like green fire.

She trusted him.

57

Her singing never ceased.

Prince Barefoot began to run on tiptoe towards the door.

Then it happened!

His bare foot struck against a splinter on the golden floor, and the tiny sliver of gold penetrated his heel and made him cry out and stumble.

He dropped the golden cage.

The bird screamed.

In a flash, the King was awake, the man with the spear was awake, the men in knots on the floor were awake, and the man asleep in the lentil soup was coming round also.

Barefoot snatched up the golden cage with the startled bird still in it. He dived for the door. He was out of the door and springing into the saddle of the little mare before the King and his men realised what was happening.

Off, off they galloped into the night. There were no stars but the moon was bright.

The little mare went like the wind.

Barefoot sat firm in the saddle in the middle of her back.

The King and the King's men were not far behind them. Barefoot did not look round, but he could hear the thunder of their horses' hooves.

After only a few hours they came in sight of the sea with the three islands in it.

"King's son," said the mare.

"Yes?" said Prince Barefoot.

"Look over your shoulder," said the mare, "and tell me what you see."

Barefoot looked over his shoulder.

"I see the King of the Golden Land," he shouted. "And I see all the King's men with him."

"What colour are their horses?" said the mare.

"Their horses are all black," Prince Barefoot said.

The little mare neighed.

"That's good," she said. "We can beat his black horses."

The mare crossed the sea with the three islands in it. Prince Barefoot sat tight in the saddle in the middle of her back, clutching the birdcage to his chest. The bird of the Golden Land started singing as they came up the further shore. It was not her best song. But it was some sort of song, and it cheered both horse and rider.

They rode on for nearly a month. Then they came in sight of the second sea.

"King's son," said the mare.

"What is it now?" said Prince Barefoot.

"Look back over your shoulder," said the mare, "and tell me what you see."

Barefoot looked over his shoulder.

"I see the King of the Golden Land," he shouted. "And I see all the King's men still with him."

"What colour are their horses?" said the mare.

"White," said Prince Barefoot. "Their horses are all white as snow."

The little mare neighed.

"The luck is still with us," she said. "We can beat his white horses."

The mare crossed the second sea without any bother. Prince Barefoot still sat firm in the saddle in the middle of her back. He held the birdcage higher so that he could hear the song of the bird of the Golden Land more clearly. As they came riding up the further shore of the second sea the bird began to sing more joyfully. Barefoot began to feel quite confident.

Again they rode on for nearly a month. At last they came in sight of the third and smallest sea.

"King's son," said the mare.

Prince Barefoot looked back over his shoulder.

'He's still there," he shouted. "The King of the Golden Land! What's more—he's gaining on us!"

The little mare snorted.

"Then all is lost," she said, her step faltering. "We can't beat his gold horses."

'What gold horses?" said Prince Barefoot. "There are no gold horses. The King of the Golden Land is riding a great stallion as red as fire, and all the King's men ride red horses also."

"Hurrah!" cried the mare, and she galloped on over the sea again, faster than ever. "All the same," she gasped as she galloped, "I don't understand this."

They reached the further shore and Prince Barefoot drew rein. Then the mare turned her own head and looked back across the water and saw that the King of the Golden Land and all the King's men, every single one of them mounted on a horse as red as fire, had remained on the other side of the final sea.

The little gold mare curled up her top lip as if she was laughing.

"It's his boots!" she said. "The idiot took of his boots when he went to sleep listening to the song of our friend the bird of the Golden Land."

"Boots?" said Prince Barefoot. "What difference do boots make?"

"Some people depend on them for their powers," explained the little gold mare. "Now if he had kept his magic boots on he could have kept on improving those horses until they could beat me."

Prince Barefoot looked down at his own bootless feet.

"Yes," said the mare. "There's a moral in this somewhere. But let's not worry about that. We've still got adventures ahead of us before we get you safe back to Ireland."

She swung her head about and trotted off down the twisty gold road in the direction of the castle where Prince Barefoot had first set his eyes on her.

The bird of the Golden Land was now singing so sweet and loud that Barefoot thought his own heart would burst with the joy of it. He opened the door of the golden cage and she sat on his shoulder. Once she flew down from his shoulder and for a terrible moment he thought that he had lost her. But the bird merely touched his foot where it had been wounded by the golden splinter. Her wing brushed against his heel and the flesh was mended by that swift softness. Then the bird of the Golden Land flew up again and perched on Prince Barefoot's shoulder, and sang, and sang.

She was still singing when they arrived at the castle where Barefoot had chosen the little gold mare a year and a day before. The young woman who had welcomed him then was standing outside the back door now. When she saw Barefoot and the mare and the singing bird coming, the young woman started dancing.

"So you were the right prince and you are the right prince!" she cried with delight.

She danced high.

She danced low.

She danced widdershins, her golden hair streaming.

She danced around and around the little gold mare

and Prince Barefoot standing barefoot in the stirrups and the bird of the Golden Land that was singing and singing like all summer rolled into a golden ball and given a voice that had the whole of summer's sweetness in it.

When the young woman stopped dancing she brushed back her hair and she said:

"So, little Prince No-Boots, do you know who that bird is on your shoulder?"

"I do," Barefoot said. "She's the bird of the Golden Land."

"And who is the bird of the Golden Land?" asked the woman.

Barefoot frowned. He was trying to remember something the little gold mare had told him. "Is she the Queen with the Three Crowns?" he said.

The young woman smiled.

"She is," said she. "That bird on your shoulder is the Queen with the Three Crowns. That little gold mare that you ride on is the Queen with the Two Crowns. And I am the Queen with the One Crown. We are sisters, you see. Once we ruled all the Golden Land, but now we want to leave it and live in the world above."

Prince Barefoot dismounted.

He bowed, as a prince should, to the bird and the mare and the young woman.

"Now, you see this rod?" said the young woman who was the Queen with the One Crown.

She held up a slender golden rod in her hand and to Barefoot's eyes it was as if a sunbeam flashed out from the tip of it.

"I see it," he said, wondering.

"This is a rod of enchantment," said the Queen with the One Crown. "It is the only thing in the world or under the world that will give back their true forms to those two queens, my sisters. Once I strike the bird of the Golden Land with it, she will no longer be the bird of the Golden Land as you know her, but she will be the Queen with the Three Crowns again. Once I strike the little gold mare with it, she will no longer be the little

64

gold mare as you know her, but she will be the Queen with the Two Crowns again."

Prince Barefoot stared from the bird to the mare.

The bird looked very like a bird and the mare looked very like a mare.

It was not that he disbelieved what the young woman was telling him, but he wanted to see it happen with his own eyes.

"Go on, then," he said.

So the Queen with the One Crown stepped forwards and tapped the little gold mare lightly on the head with the rod of enchantment.

The mare disappeared in a puff of gold smoke.

Standing in her place was a beautiful young woman with two crowns on her head. The crowns were wonderfully inlaid, so that they did not look silly.

Then the Queen with the One Crown turned and tapped the bird of the Golden Land lightly on the head with the rod of enchantment.

The bird disappeared with a musical note of pure gold.

Standing in her place was an even more beautiful young woman with three crowns on her head. The crowns did not look silly or extravagant, because they were so skilfully welded together with gold and diamonds.

Barefoot now noticed that the young woman who was the Queen with the one Crown did indeed have one crown on her head. Perhaps it had always been there, half-hidden by her long golden hair. But he rather thought that it had not, and that in some way its appearance had depended upon this revelation of the real nature of the little gold mare and the bird of the Golden Land.

The Queen with the Three Crowns spoke. Her voice was as sweet and as magical as her song had been when she was in the form of a bird.

"My dear sister the Queen with the One Crown has not told you something important about that rod," she said. "It is indeed a rod of great enchantment, but now that I am in my right form again I do not need it. I am the Queen with the Three Crowns, and the most magic of the three of us. I have it in my power to make a bird of myself whenever it pleases me."

Prince Barefoot nodded.

He knew it was rude to nod, but to tell you the truth he found the Queen with the Three Crowns so beautiful that his tongue was tied in little knots and he could not say anything sensible at all.

The Queen with the Two Crowns smiled when she realised his predicament. She spoke next:

"Three Crowns is indeed the most magic of us all," she said. "Neither One Crown nor myself has the power to change our form without the rod of enchantment."

"I see," stuttered Barefoot. Then, just for the sake of making conversation, he added: "Do you have to wield the rod yourselves?"

"No," said One Crown and Two Crowns together. "Anyone can change us."

The Queen with the Three Crowns was gazing at Prince Barefoot with great love in her adorable green eyes. Then she clapped her hands and shook back her hair that was even longer and more golden than her sisters'.

"Is your name really Barefoot?" she demanded.

"No, it isn't," said the youngest son of the King of Ireland.

"Well, don't be so shy! What is it then?"

"Cormac," said the youngest son of the King of Ireland.

"Cormac," repeated the Queen with the Three Crowns thoughtfully. "I like Cormac. Cormac is a fine name. Now, Prince Cormac, what do you think we should do next?"

Hearing himself addressed by his proper name by the most beautiful woman he had ever seen gave Barefoot more courage and confidence than he had ever felt in his life.

"I think," he said, taking the hand of the Queen with the Three Crowns, "that we should get married, you and I." Then he blushed, remembering his former bashful ways. "That is," he added, "if you will have me."

"I will," said the Queen with the Three Crowns.

And she kissed him.

And he kissed her in return.

The Queen with the Two Crowns said:

"That's all very nice and romantic, I must say. But what about me?"

Prince Cormac thought for a moment.

Then he said:

"You could marry my eldest brother. He's not a bad fellow on the whole. He's tall as a clock tower and he wears red boots."

"I think your judgement of people is a little too generous," murmured the Queen with the Three Crowns. "All the same, that Red Boots *will* inherit half of Ireland, so I suppose you could do worse, dear sister."

68

"Very well," said the Queen with the Two Crowns.

The Queen with the One Crown sniffed. "Which leaves me with the middle son of the King of Ireland, doesn't it? And is there *anything* good anyone ever said about him?"

Cormac tried hard to think of something.

"He's got a nice shiny pair of black boots," he said at last.

"And a tongue as sarcastic as sandpaper," said the Queen with the One Crown. "Oh well," she sighed. "At least he'll inherit the other half of Ireland, for what that's worth."

"For magical persons," observed the Queen with the Three Crowns, "you two are disgracefully money-minded."

"No, we're not," said the Queen with the Two Crowns. "We've just got a sense of humour, that's all."

"And a sense of proportion," added the Queen with the One Crown.

The Queen with the Three Crowns laughed. She was still holding Prince Cormac by the hand. Now she squeezed it. "I have a sense of humour and proportion too," she said. "You won't mind if I call you my little Prince Barefoot now and again, not often, but just for old times' sake?"

"Not at all," said Cormac. "Going through life without boots on has no doubt been good for me."

69

They gazed into each other's eyes.

Then:

"Enough of this love and philosophy," said the Queen with the One Crown briskly. "It's high time we all went up the long black hole to Ireland. The old man and your two brothers will have been waiting up there for a year and a day."

"Maybe they'll have given up and gone home," said Cormac.

"I don't think so," said the Queen with the One Crown wisely. "Everyone always waits for a year and a day. *Then* they give up and go home."

So they set out together along the straight gold road, Prince Cormac and the Queen with the Three Crowns dancing first, and then the Queen with the Two Crowns and the Queen with the One Crown dancing along together just behind them. And in no time at all they arrived at the bottom of the long black hole that led up into Ireland.

"After you, sister," said the Queen with the Three Crowns to the Queen with the Two Crowns. "You are to marry the eldest son of the King of Ireland, that tall Red Boots, so it's only fair that you go up first."

The Queen with the Two Crowns nodded. She gathered up her gown and stepped into the wicker basket.

Prince Cormac tugged hard on the rope that was still hanging down the hole, so that those above knew that

70

someone was wanting to come up.

Now Black Boots, the sarcastic one, had turned his back on the hole and was just about to give up and go home, because he had worked it out that the year and a day had passed, and he thought the whole adventure was over. Besides, he had never really believed in the bird of the Golden Land, and regarded even their waiting by the hole as just an excuse to indulge his natural talent for laziness.

Red Boots was turning aside to join his brother when he noticed the rope twitch.

"Hang on!" he cried. "We've caught something!"

Black Boots spun around.

The old man leaned forwards eagerly and peered at

71

the rope with his misty short-sighted eyes.

The rope twitched again.

"Pull it up!" shouted the old man. "Pull it up! Pull it up!"

So they joined forces, Red Boots, Black Boots, and the skinny old man, and they pulled and they pulled, and slowly but surely they drew the wicker basket up the long black hole in the middle of Ireland, and out stepped the Queen with the Two Crowns.

"Good morning," she said.

"Good morning," they replied.

"I'm marrying you," she said to Red Boots.

She gave him her most beautiful smile.

"Thanks," he said, and for once in his life he meant it.

Black Boots scowled horribly. "We wait a year and a day and all we get is a wife for *you*," he complained. "It's not fair."

The Queen with the Two Crowns considered this short sarcastic fellow with a critical eye. Then she shrugged her lovely shoulders. "There are more where I come from," she said. "Let down the basket!"

So they let down the wicker basket once more and then Red Boots, Black Boots, and the skinny old man joined forces, and they pulled and they pulled, and slowly but surely they drew it again up the long black hole in the middle of Ireland, and out stepped the Queen with the One Crown.

"Morning," she said.

"Morning," they replied.

"I'm marrying you," she said to Black Boots.

She gave him her most beautiful smile, although he was not much to look at.

Black Boots could hardly believe his luck.

"Thanks," he said, and for once in his life he *almost* meant it.

Now the Queen with the One Crown said:

"There are more where we came from."

"Such as who?" demanded Black Boots suspiciously.

"Such as your nice little brother with no boots," said the Queen with the One Crown.

"And such as our sister with the Three Crowns who is going to marry him," added the Queen with the Two Crowns.

Red Boots and Black Boots looked at each other.

It was a very sly look.

The old man rubbed his hands together with fiendish glee when he saw that look, though the two Queens were startled by the slyness of it.

However, the Queens had no choice if they wanted Cormac and the Queen with the Three Crowns to join them, so the two women could only watch as Red Boots and Black Boots and the eager old man lowered the empty wicker basket down the long black hole.

It reached the bottom.

Prince Cormac held out his hand to help the Queen

73

with the Three Crowns to step into it.

"Wait a bit," she whispered. "Do you trust your brothers?"

Cormac remembered how Red Boots and Black Boots had always despised him. How they had not cared when he had to go barefoot while they wore the only boots ever made by the royal bootmaker. How they had lowered him down the hole at such a great rate that he had been pitched out of the basket.

"I don't know if I trust them," he said at last. "I don't know if I know enough about human nature at all."

The Queen with the Three Crowns smiled. "Then you are learning about human nature fast," she said. "And that is good."

"But if a man cannot trust his own brothers, then who *can* he trust?" Cormac asked.

"Start with yourself," advised the Queen with the Three Crowns. "And then go on to any woman who has it in her power to turn into a golden bird."

And so saying, she rolled away a big stone that was lying against the wall at the bottom of the pit, and she got Cormac to help her place it in the wicker basket.

Then she called up the hole in her sweetest voice: "We're ready!"

Red Boots and Black Boots rubbed their hands. Then they started pulling up the basket. The skinny old man was cackling with glee as he tried to help

74

them—but they brushed him aside. "Leave this to us," they said. They pulled and they pulled. The stone was heavy and the sweat poured down their faces. "Barefoot's put on weight," grunted Red Boots. "And his bride-to-be must be as fat as a pig," sneered Black Boots. However, they did not intend to see Barefoot or his bride-to-be in any case. For as soon as the wicker basket was about three quarters of the way up the long black hole in the middle of Ireland, Red Boots drew his sword and slashed right through the rope.

The basket went back down the hole at a frightful rate. And hit the bottom with a bang.

The ground trembled under the feet of Red Boots, Black Boots, the old man, and the two Queens left standing at the top.

Red Boots laughed. "Bye, bye, Barefoot," he said.

Black Boots joined in the laughter. "He always had it coming to him," he said. And turning to the Queen with the One Crown and the Queen with the Two Crowns, he added: "Don't look so gloomy, girls!

75

Getting rid of that pair means there's all the more of Ireland left for us."

Red Boots and Black Boots now set out for home. The Queen with the One Crown and the Queen with the Two Crowns walked along behind them, casting sad looks back over their shoulders, but unable to do anything about the situation. The skinny old man came last of all in the little procession. He seemed well pleased with the way things had turned out. A crafty light was beginning to sharpen his misty eyes, so that he looked even more devilish.

After a while, the old man skipped ahead and tugged at Red Boots' sleeve. Red Boots tried to brush him away impatiently. But the old man drew the tall prince aside into the shadow of a dark oak tree.

"You're forgetting something," he whispered. "In fact, you've forgotten the most important thing of all."

"What's that?" demanded Red Boots.

"The bird of the Golden Land," said the old man.

Red Boots snorted. "I don't believe in the bird of the Golden Land."

"But your father the King of Ireland believes in the bird of the Golden Land," the old man pointed out cunningly. "And it was the bird of the Golden Land he set you out to look for."

Black Boots had overheard the conversation. "Look," he said. "Does it matter? We've got a wife each which is what we wanted. And we've got rid of that little monster Barefoot. Our father can divide the kingdom between the two of us."

"But his crown is worth more than the kingdom," said the old man. "And he promised to give that crown, which is so much more valuable than Ireland, only to the son who would bring him back the bird of the Golden Land."

"That's true," mused Red Boots.

"So how can we bring him something that doesn't exist?" said Black Boots.

The old man winked his greedy eye. "For a suitable reward," he promised, "I will tell you what to do."

Red Boots and Black Boots consulted each other.

Red Boots nodded.

Black Boots shrugged.

They agreed they would reward him if he could really help them. (Privately, each of them was thinking that the "reward" would be something like a sharp shove off the top of a cliff in Connemara.)

"That Queen with the One Crown," hissed the old man. "See that rod in her right hand? Well, I've seen rods like that before. It's what they call a rod of enchantment. It turns things into other things."

Red Boots sneaked a look at the golden rod in the hand of the Queen with the One Crown. "Wait a bit," he said. "If that's true, why doesn't she change herself into something else and escape?"

"The world of enchantment is not so simple as you

suppose," explained the old man. "There are rules and limits and degrees. Don't I know! The Queen with the One Crown has the power to change others, but no power to change herself. It's the same with the Queen with the Two Crowns. Only the Queen with the Three Crowns can change back and forth on her own as she pleases."

Red Boots chuckled and rubbed his hands. "And she is now dead at the bottom of the long black hole," he observed with evident satisfaction. "So I don't think we'll be seeing any change for the better in her!"

"Quick!" cried Black Boots, leaping forwards.

For the Queen with the One Crown had plainly guessed the drift of what they were plotting under the dark oak, and she had raised the rod of enchantment in her hand and was about to touch her sister lightly on the top of the head with it.

Black Boots grabbed the Queen with the One Crown before she could bring the rod down. Then the old man, leaping like an eel, had the rod out of the Queen's hand. He spun. He twisted. Red Boots seized the Queen with the Two Crowns. The old man brought the rod down on her head. And as he brought it down, the old man cried in a loud and terrible voice:

"Change! Change! Change! *Change into the bird of the Golden Land in her cage!*"

All at once, there was an explosion of gold and diamonds and the Queen with the Two Crowns disappeared.

In her place, dangling from Red Boots' right hand, was a gilded cage with a bird in it. The bird had deep green eyes and feathers of the most brilliant and glossy gold.

"Not bad," said Red Boots.

Then he thought for a bit.

"Mind you," he added, "I've gained a bird and lost a wife."

The old man corrected him:

"Sir," he said, "you have gained a bird and lost a wife—and gained the crown of Ireland!"

"Hmmm," said Red Boots. "It's a reasonable deal."

Black Boots was looking thoughtfully at the tips of his black boots. He was wondering if things were going to turn out anywhere near as well for him. All the same, he held his tongue for the time being.

He cheered up considerably when the old man handed him the rod of enchantment, saying:

"You'd better hold on to that. Keep it from the woman you are going to marry for a start. Otherwise you might wake up one morning with antennae on your head, or frog's legs."

Black Boots stuck the rod down the inside of his left black boot.

The party travelled on towards the castle of the King of Ireland.

When they came in sight of it they saw that it was as

full of cobwebs as ever. The flags were rotting on the
flagpoles. The moat was full of sedge and old bottles.
The drawbridge had collapsed and they had to make
their way into the castle keep across a plank. The
sentries had not shaved for months.

The King of Ireland came out to meet them. He
looked haggard and woe-begone.

"I haven't slept for a year and a day," he said. "I
kept lying awake waiting for that bird of the Golden
Land."

All the same, his face brightened up when he saw his
two sons, Red Boots and Black Boots, and he hugged
them and kissed them, and welcomed them home. "I'll

have the window-sills painted now you're back," he said.

Then he looked round the little group, counting them, and kissing the hand of the Queen with the One Crown, who had not yet spoken a word. "Wait a bit," he said, "where is your brother? Where's Prince Cormac? My dear little Barefoot?"

"Oh *him*," said Red Boots. "That was sad . . . "

"Sad?"

"A rock fell and crushed him on the road," said Black Boots. "Made a terrible mess too."

A single tear ran down the face of the King of Ireland. When another tear appeared in his other eye, Red Boots held up the gilded cage with the bird in it.

"Look, father!" he said.

The King of Ireland stared at the bird through his tears. He did not know whether to laugh or cry. "And to think that I desired that bird more than anything else in the world," he murmured. "Yet now I would give a hundred such birds to have my own little Barefoot back . . ."

Red Boots' face got as red as his boots. "I risked life and limb to get you this bird," he lied. "And now you spurn her? I'm your son too, remember. Do you mean you're not grateful? Do I not get the crown as you promised? Is it all a cheat?"

The King his father dried his tears with a big silk royal handkerchief. He did his best to rejoice that at

81

least the bird was now his.

He shook Red Boots by the hand and thanked him warmly.

Then he hung the cage with the bird in it on the hook by his bedside.

The King went to bed.

He looked at the bird and waited.

The bird looked at him.

The bird shut her eyes and hid her head under her wing.

The King sat propped up amongst the royal pillows all night, but the bird did not sing.

Towards dawn, bleary eyed, the King tiptoed over to the cage and stuck his forefinger through the bars and tickled the bird's beak. The bird promptly bit him.

The King snatched up the gilded cage with the bird in it and stalked down to the throne room.

Red Boots, Black Boots, and the old man were waiting for him there. So was the Queen with the One Crown.

"You fool!" thundered the King of Ireland at his eldest son. "This is not the bird of the Golden Land!"

"Of course it is!" blustered Red Boots. "Didn't I journey to the Golden Land and bring her back for you despite all hardships and dangers?" He turned to appeal to his brother, Black Boots. "Tell him the truth," he ordered.

Black Boots seized his chance to get the crown of

82

Ireland all for himself.

"All right," he said in a loud clear voice. "I'll tell the truth since you ask me, dear brother." He turned to his father and bowed with pretended respect. "That bird in the cage you hold in your hand is *not* the bird of the Golden Land!"

"I knew it!" cried the King. "So you failed? You both failed?" He stamped up and down the throne room, kicking at the throne. "Very well, then," he concluded, "neither of you will get the crown. I will sell it to the French and go to live in Paris on the proceeds!"

Black Boots took the rod of enchantment from the inside of his left boot.

"Father," he said. "Don't be so melodramatic! Ireland needs a King. Ireland needs a crown."

His father was in no mood to listen to speeches like this. He took a running jump at his throne and kicked it over.

"Ireland needs only one thing!" he shouted. "Ireland needs the bird of the Golden Land!"

Black Boots smiled.

He crossed swiftly to the Queen with the One Crown.

He struck her with the rod of enchantment.

"Change! Change! Change!" he chanted. "*Change into the bird of the Golden Land!*"

All at once, in a puff of gold smoke and pearls, the Queen with the One Crown disappeared.

83

In her place, dangling from Black Boots' right hand, was a gilded cage with a bird in it. The bird had deep green eyes and feathers of the most brilliant and glossy gold.

The King of Ireland looked from the bird held by Black Boots to the bird held by Red Boots.

There was silence in the throne room for the space of half an hour.

Then the King said:

"Sing!"

Neither bird made a sound. Their little green eyes looked at each other mischievously.

"Sing!" said the King of Ireland, louder. "Sing! Sing! Any old thing! It doesn't have to be a rhapsody, you know. Not even a madrigal. Or an Irish jig. I just want music! The bird of the Golden Land, the *real* bird of the Golden Land, that bird could sing like nothing that ever before had been heard on earth or for all I know in heaven either! And here come you two cheats bringing me birds that haven't got a squeak so spare between them! Do you think I'm a fool? Is this the way you treat your father? Give me that rod! *Give me that rod!*"

And, so saying, the King of Ireland seized the rod of enchantment where it had fallen from the hand of his son Black Boots and gave him a hefty whack with it over the head. He caught his son Red Boots too, and gave him an equally hefty whack. Fortunately for them, the rod of enchantment had no power to change the person it struck unless the striker uttered words as he did the striking. And the King of Ireland was so choked with fury at being cheated by his sons that he said nothing as he hit them. So they were only bruised.

But then the King of Ireland got his breath back, and as he got his breath back he noticed the old man standing in the corner watching all these antics with an evil leer on his face.

"You!" roared the King. "I know you're somewhere at the bottom of this! Why, you're nothing better than a heap of dust, are you? Devil! Devil! Dust! Dust!"

He struck the old man three times over the skull with the rod of enchantment.

The old man howled. It was not just the howl of an old man. It was the howl of a devil returning to what he was.

Then there was *no* old man standing before the King of Ireland.

Instead, there was a little heap of black ashes on the

floor of the throne room.

And there was a dirty black smear of ash on the tip of the rod of enchantment.

The King of Ireland was so frightened at what he had done that he hurled the rod into the fire, where it started to burn with a slow gold flame.

Meanwhile, back at the bottom of the long black hole in the middle of Ireland, the Queen with the Three Crowns had been busy making a bird of herself.

Her eyes got greener and greener.

Feathers grew out of her skin and the feathers got golder and golder.

Wings sprouted from her shoulders.

At last the transformation was complete.

The Queen with the Three Crowns had turned once more into the bird of the Golden Land.

As soon as she was a bird again, she flew up the long black hole and came out into Ireland.

It was raining.

A soft, clinging rain, such as it often rains in Ireland.

The bird of the Golden Land shook the soft clinging rain from her feathers. She did not sing. She had too much on her mind for singing. Instead, she stood quite still in the rain and concentrated on turning herself back into a woman again.

Her wings shrank. Then they disappeared.

Her feathers melted. Soon it was just as if she had never been covered with feathers, only with lovely golden skin.

You could only have recognised her by her eyes. They were still very green and clear and sparkled like the sea in the morning when the sun shines on it.

Otherwise, the bird of the Golden Land was gone.

And in her place stood the Queen with the Three Crowns.

Now, when she flew up the hole in the form of the bird she had held in her beak the end of the rope that had been tied to the wicker basket. It was a matter of only a few minutes to attach this half of the rope firmly to the half that remained at the top, where Red Boots had cut it with his sword.

"Cormac," she cried down the hole.

"Yes, my love?"

"Climb into the wicker basket."

"I can't," said Cormac. "It's all smashed. When the basket with that big stone in it hit the bottom of the hole the sides of the basket burst."

The Queen with the Three Crowns thought quickly.

Then she started whistling. It was a very high-pitched whistle and it sounded over every mountain and echoed throughout every valley in that part of Ireland. All at once the air was filled with the thunder of powerful wings. Golden eagles and silver swans were thronging towards the Queen with the Three Crowns where she stood with her arms outstretched to welcome them.

"Cormac, my dear little Prince Barefoot," she called down the hole.

"Yes, my love?"

"I want you to untie your end of the rope from the handles of the wicker basket."

Prince Cormac did so.

"Now tie the rope round your waist as tight as you can," instructed the Queen with the Three Crowns.

"I've done that!"

"And hold on to the rope a little bit over your head."

"I've done that too!"

"Very good," said the Queen with the Three Crowns. "Now here comes the tricky bit. I'm going to pull you up the hole."

Prince Cormac cried out protesting. "You'll never manage it! I'm too heavy! Look, I don't mind so much falling and being dashed to pieces on the rocks down here. But you'll fall down after me and be dashed to bits too!"

"Trust me," said the Queen with the Three Crowns simply.

Then she tied her end of the long coil of rope around her own slender waist and she beckoned to the golden eagles and the silver swans. The birds came thronging. They made a chariot of their gold and silver wings and the Queen with the Three Crowns stepped into the winged chariot.

"Are you ready, love?" she called down to Cormac.

88

"Yes, but—"

The Queen with the Three Crowns snapped her fingers.

Then:

"Up, eagles! Up, swans! Up, up, and away!" she cried.

And the eagles and the swans lifted her slowly and gently into the soft Irish air.

It was still raining, and as the eagles and the swans bore the Queen higher and higher she got wetter and wetter, until her long golden hair was sticking to her face and shoulders.

But the Queen did not care. For slowly but surely Prince Cormac was being drawn up the long black hole. The rope twisted tight about the Queen's waist did not hurt her so very much either, because Cormac was able to work his way up the sides of the hole using his bare feet to scrabble at crannies and bear some of his weight. "I knew there would be some use in having gone through life so far without boots," he said happily to himself, as he realised how he must be helping her to bear the strain.

At last, Prince Cormac reached the top.

His hands grasped the edges of the hole.

The swans and the eagles, with the Queen in the chariot of their powerful wings, hovered above him.

Then, with a final heave, he rolled himself over the edge and out onto good Irish ground again. That ground was soaking wet with the rain which was still falling, but Cormac kissed the ground, wet as it was, and rolled about in the mud. He was so glad to be back in the real world!

The Queen with the Three Crowns whistled three times and stroked the necks of the eagles and swans. They lowered her to the ground. She undid the rope from about her waist and waved them goodbye as they flew away back to their mountains and lakes.

She kissed Prince Cormac.

He kissed her in return.

"You," she said, "are rather muddy."

"Sorry," he said, undoing the rope from around his own middle.

"That's quite all right," she said. "To tell you the truth, a Queen can get tired and bored of too much gold and cleanliness. A little Irish mud is good for the soul."

They set out together in the direction of the castle of the King of Ireland. When they got there and entered the throne room they saw an amazing sight.

Prince Red Boots was on his knees beside a little gilded cage. He was making chirping noises in a desperate effort to get the bird in the cage to sing. The bird was staring into space with an expression of icy and unalterable boredom in its eyes. Not a squeak came from its beak.

A few yards away, on the other side of the throne,

91

Prince Black Boots was reading a fat book called *Teach Yourself Magic*. Every now and again he jumped up and waved his hands over another little bird in another gilded cage, muttering all sorts of gibberish . The bird did not even look at him.

Both birds looked up when the Queen with the Three Crowns walked in, however. And their little green eyes opened wide and bright with delight when they saw Prince Cormac with her.

The King of Ireland was sitting miserably on his throne and staring at a heap of dust on the ground in front of him. From time to time he stirred the dust with his foot, and murmured, "To hell with it!"

"I'm afraid that's just about where it is," said the Queen with the Three Crowns.

"It?" said the King of Ireland.

"It," said the Queen with the Three Crowns. "He looked like a skinny old man but he was really a very wicked magician. He was the one who first opened up that long black hole in the middle of Ireland. He intended to get down to hell, but he took the wrong turning. After that, he was forever getting his own back by luring lost travellers down there."

The King of Ireland shrugged. He looked more worried and woe-begone than ever.

"Oh drat and pickles! To hell with hell!" he said crossly. "And to hell with the Golden Land too!"

"If I were you, I wouldn't say that," the Queen with

the Three Crowns murmured sweetly. "They're quite separate places, you know."

"Are they now?" demanded the King. "And who the drat are you, madam? And what the pickles do you know about it?" He blinked and rubbed the tears from his eyes. He could not quite be sure if his own tears were dazzling him, or if this woman was really the most incredible vision of loveliness he had ever seen. To take his mind off the problem, he glanced at the mud-covered rascal standing next to her. "And what is this dratty pickled thing you've brought in with you?" he went on irritably. "I know Ireland is a poor country and my castle is full of cobwebs and the moat is full of empty bottles and now we've even got devils turning into dust all over the place, but there is a *limit*, by golly, by drat, by pickles, and . . ."

"Hullo, Dad," said Prince Barefoot.

The King of Ireland rubbed his eyes.

But now he could not stop the tears from blinding them.

"Please don't mock me," he begged, sobbing. "My youngest and dearest son was killed. He was crushed by a rock on the road. I sent him off in search of the bird of the Golden Land that I thought was the joy of my heart. He died on that quest, and now all I have left in the world are these two fraudulent bird-fanciers."

He stabbed his finger in the direction of Red Boots and Black Boots, still crouched by their cages and

93

trying to coax the mute little birds to sing.

But Red Boots, for his part, and Black Boots, for his part, now started to crawl at some speed towards the door. No tears were blinding their eyes. They could see what was coming.

Barefoot wiped the mud from his cheeks and his forehead.

The Queen with the Three Crowns kissed away the last smudge of it from his nose.

"Hullo, Dad," said Barefoot again.

His father could not believe it.

Then he could!